SHOES

by Elizabeth Winthrop
Illustrated by William Joyce

HarperTrophy
A Division of HarperCollins*Publishers*

For Vajra and Vasundhara, with love
E.W.

To my good friend, Mary Long
B.J.

Shoes
Text copyright © 1986 by Elizabeth Winthrop Mahony
Illustrations copyright © 1986 by William Joyce
Printed in the U.S.A.   All rights reserved.
Designed by Pat Tobin

Library of Congress Cataloging-in-Publication Data
Winthrop, Elizabeth.
   Shoes.

   Summary: A survey of the many kinds of shoes in the
world concludes that the best of all are the perfect
natural shoes that are your feet.
   [1. Shoes—Fiction.   2. Foot—Fiction.   3. Stories
in rhyme]   I. Joyce, William, ill.   II. Title.
PZ8.3.W727Sh   1986   [E]   85-45841
ISBN 0-06-026591-4
ISBN 0-06-026592-2 (lib. bdg.)

   (A Harper Trophy book)
ISBN 0-06-443171-1 (pbk.)

First Harper Trophy edition, 1988.

SHOES

There are shoes to buckle, shoes to tie,

shoes too low,

and shoes too high.

Shoes to run in, shoes for sliding,

high-topped shoes for horseback riding.

Shoes too loose, shoes too tight,

shoes to snuggle in at night.

Shoes to skate in, shoes to skip in,

shoes to turn a double flip in.

Shoes for fishing, shoes for wishing,

rubber shoes for muddy squishing.

11

Shoes with ribbons, shoes with bows,

shoes to skate in when it snows.

Shoes for winter, shoes for fall,

shoes for spring, but best of all…

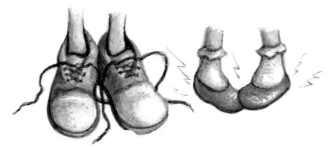

They're not too loose and not too tight.

They can be worn both day and night.

They're right for chasing, right for racing,

no time lost in silly lacing.

They will not pinch or raise a blister

or get passed down to Baby Sister.

Perfect fit, very neat,

made especially for the heat—

your very own skinny-boned, wiggly-toed

FEET.

URBANA

URBANA